First American Edition 2020
Kane Miller, A Division of EDC Publishing

First published in Great Britain 2019 by Alanna Max,
38 Oakfield Road, London N4 4NL, UK.
Where's Lenny? copyright © Alanna Max 2019
Text and illustrations copyright © Ken Wilson-Max 2019
The moral rights of the author/illustrator have been asserted.

For information contact:
Kane Miller, A Division of EDC Publishing
P.O. Box 470663
Tulsa, OK 74147-0663
www.kanemiller.com
www.edcpub.com
www.usbornebooksandmore.com

Library of Congress Control Number: 2019943618

Printed and bound in China
1 2 3 4 5 6 7 8 9 10
ISBN: 978-1-68464-070-6
Illustrated with acrylic.

Ken Wilson-Max

Where's Lenny?

Kane Miller

A DIVISION OF EDC PUBLISHING

There goes Lenny,
playing hide-and-seek.

Here's Daddy, counting
and singing ...

Daddy counts:

"1 2 3 4 5

Once I caught a fish alive.

6 7 8 9 10

Then I let it go again.

Where's Lenny?

Daddy hears a rumbling in the cupboard.

"Aha!" he says.
But when he opens
the door he finds nothing.

Where's Lenny?

"Aha!" he says.
But it's only Mommy.

Where's Lenny?
Daddy sees something
by the window.

"Aha!" he says.
But it's only Wilbur,
wagging his tail.

Where's Lenny?
Daddy hears
a bubbling noise,
but it's only Gordon
the goldfish.

Where's Lenny?

**Daddy sees blobs of jam
and follows them
up the stairs.**

Where's Lenny?

Daddy hears tap, tap, tap in the bathroom.

"Aha!" he says.
But it's only Mommy,
fixing the light.

Where's Lenny?

Mommy and Daddy
rush into Lenny's room.

"Aha!"
they say.
But no one
is there.

Then they hear a giggle.
Mommy and Daddy creep toward
the little giggly bump in the bed and ...

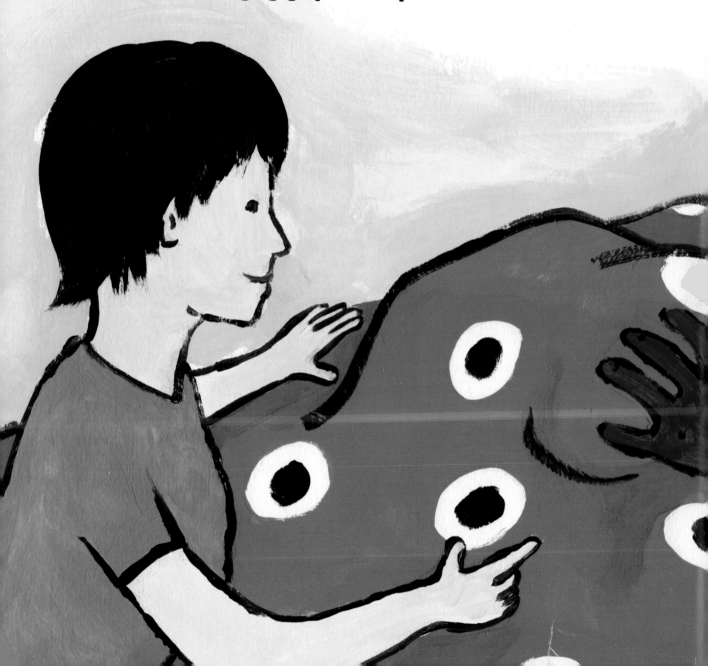

"Aha!" says Daddy.

Here's Lenny!

Here are
Mommy and Daddy
with Lenny,

tickling and tickling,
laughing and hugging.